Miss Crump's
Funny Bone

To Reagan —
Read for
laughs!
Rachelle Burk

by Rachelle Burk
illustrations by Rex Schneider

Miss Crump's Funny Bone
Text copyright © 2015 Rachelle Burk.
Illustrations copyright © 2015 by Rex Schneider.

WiggleRoom Books
11 Brookhill Road, East Brunswick, NJ 08816
WiggleRoomBooks@gmail.com

ISBN: 978-0692531204

Printed in the USA

For Fred,
who knows how to tickle my funny bone.

Chapter 1

On the door to Mrs. Greenberg's classroom is a dancing book and a sign announcing, "Explore and Soar!"

The walls inside are covered with
posters of space shuttles and
galaxies. There is an ant farm, a
garden snake that eats live

crickets, and a gerbil named Verb who gnaws wooden toys to bits.

It's the coolest class in all of Lakeview Elementary School.

Unfortunately, it's not mine.

When the morning bell rings, I drag myself next door to Miss Crump's third grade class. In here, the walls are covered with posters listing rules for good behavior. And instead of cool animals, we have a droopy bean plant left over from an old science project. When we asked Miss Crump if we could have a pet like Mrs. Greenberg's class, she cringed. "I don't much care for hoppy-crawly things," she said. She rubbed her chin and added, "However, you may bring in models of endangered species, if you like."

Now we have a droopy bean plant and a dumb plastic polar bear.

This morning, Miss Crump stood at the door like a police officer, making sure we hung our jackets neatly. She didn't notice Connor McGiblin putting his glasses on the polar bear. When she finally saw it, she stood with her hands on her hips and said, "I fail to find the humor in that."

From what I can tell, Grumpy Crumpy fails to find the humor in anything. Like last week, two clowns came to school and did a bunch of funny skits for Fire Safety Month. One clown couldn't remember "stop, drop, and roll" and instead did "hop, mop, and bowl." The whole audience cracked up. All except Miss Crump. She sat there the entire time checking her fingernails and picking lint off her skirt. Even real live clowns couldn't get a chuckle out of her.

But this morning, after Miss Crump took attendance, we finally thought we saw her smile. Joanna Mertz had brought in a batch of her homemade muffins. They were kind of lopsided and a weird gray color, though they smelled pretty good.

"Try one, Miss Crump. It's my own secret recipe," Joanna said. Miss Crump always says she "encourages originality." That means she likes you to make stuff yourself. To prove she means it, she tried Joanna's muffin. First she took a deep breath, followed by a big, slow bite.

As she chewed, her mouth actually turned up on the sides. We could hardly believe our eyes. Was it really happening?

"Look! She's smiling!" someone shouted. I wasn't so sure. Miss Crump's eyes got big and round, with the stunned look of someone who stepped barefoot in dog poop. She covered her mouth and ran to spit in the sink. If that was a smile, I say it doesn't count.

The muffin crisis only made Miss Crump grumpier. She paced in front of the room like a dog on a chain, snapping at everyone. "Raul, if you can't sit still in your chair, I'm going to make you stand! Corrie, move your backpack before someone trips!" She called on kids who didn't have their hands up so she could scold them for not being prepared. By ten o'clock, when art class rolled around, we couldn't wait to get out of the room. A couple kids knocked over their chairs racing for the door.

"Children!" Miss Crump huffed. "You will line up when I say so, and in an orderly manner.

Do I need to tell you this every time?" She made us return to our seats before ordering us to line up by rows.

As we stood in single file at the door, my best friend Jeffrey Scott put his arm around my shoulder. "Frankie, we're in a slump, and that has to change."

"A slump?" I asked. "What kind of slump?"

"A grump slump. And we're going to do something about it."

He wouldn't say another word, even as he walked behind me down the hall. "Too many ears," he whispered to the back of my head. It's true. The place was crawling with teachers and hall monitors.

I didn't know exactly what Jeffrey had in mind, but I started to sweat. I had a feeling something big was going to happen.

Chapter 2

Twice a week, we get a break from Miss Crump when we have art class with Mr. Picaso. That's no joke—his name is really Mr. Picaso, like the famous painter, only it's spelled with one "s" instead of two. He says it's only a coincidence, but I bet if his name was Mr. Flush he might have become a plumber instead of an art teacher.

This morning he taught a lesson in watercolor painting. "Here is a fact that not everyone knows," he said in his pretend-serious voice. "Pablo Picasso's 'Blue Period' was followed by his 'Goofy Period.' Today we will study the master, and paint in the style of Pablo's Goofy Period."

Mr. Picaso perched on a stool in front of the room, with crayons sticking out of his nostrils. "Be creative," he instructed. "Let your muse run wild!"

That's his way of saying, "use your imagination." For half an hour, he sat as still as a statue. Everyone giggled as we painted his portrait.

Next to me, Jeffrey dipped his brush in the paint and dabbed it on his canvas. "Hey Frankie," he whispered, "don't you think school would be so much better if Miss Crump's class was more like this?"

"Yeah, like that would ever happen."

"We'll see about that," he said with a gleam in his eyes.

My eyes narrowed. "What kind of trouble are you planning, Jeffrey?"

"Ohhh, nothing," he sang. But his silly grin told me something else.

He went back to his portrait. "We'll talk later," he said. "For now, we paint."

Near the end of the class period, Mr. Picaso sneezed out the green crayon and walked around to admire our work. First, he looked at Alana Song's paper. Her painting showed Mr. Picaso as a dragon, with crayons pouring out of his nose like flames. It was really cool. In fact, everything about Alana is cool. She's got this cute dimple and always smells like butter cookies. I stared over at her and her painting. Like usual, she never looked my way.

Mr. Picaso moved to the next student. "Jeffrey! This is very interesting. Can you explain the meaning behind your creation?"

"Well, I made the crayons falling from your nose in cracked up pieces, because you really crack me up!" The kids all laughed. Mr. Picaso chuckled and patted Jeffrey's shoulder.

Finally, he came around to my desk.

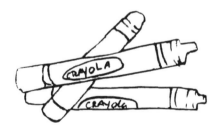

"Frank, nice use of metaphor!" He held up my painting for the class to see. "Notice how he has not only painted crayons in my nose, but in my ears and mouth as well. Through his painting, Frank is saying that all of our senses add color to our lives!"

Really? I said that? Let me tell you, that man is a genius when it comes to art.

I beamed proudly and glanced over at Jeffrey. I could tell he hadn't been listening. And by the look on his face, I knew he was busy scheming.

Chapter 3

The only bad thing about Mr. Picaso's art class is that it has to end. Then it's back to the gloominess of Grumpy Crumpy. Today she'd been crankier than ever as we watched a video Spanish lesson. She sat behind her cluttered desk, twisting side to side in her swivel chair and scanning the room for gum chewers and note passers.

"Alex!" she snapped, "Spit that out! Preeta, if I see you passing one more note you'll be taking a note from me to Mr. Kropp's office." She let out a loud sigh and shook her head, as if Alex and Preeta were bad puppies who wet the rug. All we could do was deal with it, and count the minutes until lunch period.

Jeffrey wore a smirk on his face all the way to the lunchroom. We sat down with our friend Lovey Miller. Lovey's real name is Olivia, but her baby sister couldn't pronounce it, and it came out "Lovey." Even though the baby is now seven years old, the name stuck.

Jeffrey leaned in close to me and Lovey across the table, with trouble written all over his face. I was finally going to find out what he was up to.

"Bet you guys can't get Miss Crump to laugh," he said in a hushed I-dare-you voice.

"Oh, like you can?" said Lovey. She sank her teeth into her veggie wrap.

"I bet I can," Jeffrey boasted. "Somebody needs to! That class is too depressing. I'd rather spend every day in jail, or with no TV…or in jail with no TV! What do you say? Whoever can get Miss Crump to laugh, wins."

"I don't know about this," I said. A queasy feeling in my stomach told me this was a bad idea. My stomach is usually right. Jeffrey's bets and dares have landed us in detention once or twice, after I ignored the warnings in my belly.

Jeffrey smacked his hand on the table. "Grumpiness is like a sickness. Haven't you ever heard the expression, 'Laughter is the best medicine'? We'd be doing Miss Crump a favor. C'mon, Franklin. What can go wrong by trying to cheer her up?"

"Don't call me Franklin," I sneered. My mom calls me that when she's mad. Jeffrey knows I hate it. He also knows he can usually shame me into going along with his dumb ideas, especially when Alana Song might be listening. I wouldn't want her to think I'm chicken or anything.

I glanced over at her at the end of our table. Alana spends the whole lunch period with her nose in a comic book. She's so busy giggling over the cartoons that she barely notices her lunch, much less me. I bet she would talk to me if I could make Miss Crump laugh. After all, that would practically make me a superhero. On the other hand, I might only make a big fool of myself in front of Alana. I wasn't sure it was worth the risk.

Lovey, on the other hand, seemed to consider Jeffrey's bet. "What do I get if I win—a trophy or something?" She swiped a napkin across her mouth. Lovey plans to be an Olympic gymnast when she grows up. To her, winning is everything, and if there isn't a prize in it, she loses interest pretty fast.

Jeffrey decided to make it worth her while. "No, something better." He rubbed his hands together and rummaged through his lunch bag. "How about…my sardine sandwich!"

"Gross!" Lovey crinkled her face. "That can be the loser's prize."

"What do you have, Frankie?" Jeffrey asked.

I looked over at Alana. For a second, her eyes locked with mine, like she was waiting for my answer. I emptied my lunch bag onto the table. "I'll put in my Oreos."

"Here's my gummy bears," said Lovey.

Jeffrey tossed his cheese curls into the pile. "Winner takes all."

Chapter 4

We huddled close together like football players calling the next play.

"The rules are simple," Jeffrey said. "We each get one chance to make Miss Crump laugh."

"It has to be a real laugh," I added, remembering the muffin incident.

"Yeah," agreed Jeffrey. "It's important to know the difference. Sometimes my baby brother makes this weird face and grunting noise, and you'd swear he's laughing. A minute later, my mother has to change his diaper."

Lovey rolled her eyes. "I'm sure Miss Crump is potty trained."

"Probably," Jeffrey agreed. "So, do we have a bet?" We shook on it.

"I know what I'm going to do to get her to laugh," I said. "During the science test on Friday, I'll wear the Einstein mask that I wore last Halloween. It's hysterical."

"Wait a minute," Jeffrey said, holding up a finger. "I forgot to mention one more rule: you have to make her laugh by the end of the day."

"Today? I don't have my Einstein mask here at school!"

"Sorry, it's got to be today," Jeffrey insisted. "This is an

emergency. Besides, the sardine
sandwich won't stay fresh
forever." He sniffed it. "I'm not
sure it's even fresh now."

How would I ever come up
with an idea that fast? There
were only three and a half hours
left of the school day.

"I don't know what else
would make Miss Crump laugh,"
I said, shaking my head.

"I'll show you what works
on my brother every time," said
Jeffrey. He stretched his arm
across his lips and blew hard.

PFFFFT!

The kids at the next table
giggled. Even Alana looked up
from her comic book and
grinned.

"See?" Jeffrey smiled. "It sounds like a great big…"

"Eww!" Lovey butted in. "Miss Crump will not think that's funny."

"She's right," I told Jeffrey. "Miss Crump would fail to see the humor in that."

Jeffrey wasn't convinced. "It's all how you time it. You'll see."

Lovey took another bite of

her veggie wrap and looked thoughtful. "I bet she's the kind of person who likes jokes," she said. "Educational jokes, of course—you know, being a teacher and all."

Now it was my turn to roll my eyes. "I personally don't know any educational jokes," I said. "I personally don't even know what an educational joke is. In fact, I personally don't see how something can be educational and funny at the same time."

Lovey shrugged, with that know-it-all look on her face. For a few minutes we plotted silently. I tapped my teeth with a plastic fork. Lovey twirled her hair. Jeffrey dug at his earwax. What

could possibly get Miss Crump
to laugh?

Jeffrey nudged me. "Hey,
there she is."

Lovey and I looked across
the lunchroom at the teachers'
table. Mr. Picaso shoveled down
a piece of pie while he chatted to
Miss Crump. Miss Crump only

nodded as she sipped her milk through a straw. I imagined Mr. Picaso saying something to make her laugh so hard that milk would come out of her nose like a fire hose. If there is anyone with that kind of talent, it's Mr. Picaso.

Instead, he sat there with Miss Crump, looking all dull and teacher-ish. Miss Crump has that effect on people.

Chapter 5

I barely finished eating by the time the end-of-lunch bell rang. We hurried back to class, since Grumpy Crumpy takes off points for anyone who comes back late.

I daydreamed through most of the math lesson, trying to think of something funny.

"You see," said Miss Crump, her arms waving across the board, "when you add the digits of the product, they should equal nine. That's how you know you have multiplied nine correctly!"

She got so excited about multiplication that you'd think

she was talking about a trip to Disneyland. Her eyes gleamed as they scanned the room. It looked like she expected us to stand up and cheer for the nine-times-table.

"Any questions?"

Lovey raised her hand. "I have a question."

She threw a glance at me and Jeffrey. I could tell Lovey was up to something. She stood up and tried to look serious. "Why is six afraid of seven?"

Miss Crump looked at her all confused, as if Lovey was speaking Martian.

"Excuse me?"

Lovey shuffled her feet a little. "I said, um, why is six afraid of seven?"

Miss Crump stood still and silent, with her mouth opened like a Venus flytrap.

Lovey blurted out, "Because seven ate nine!"

The kids who got it snickered. I didn't get it.

Lovey must have figured that Miss Crump didn't get it either, because she started to explain. "It's a joke, Miss Crump! Seven *eight* nine." Lovey drew a number eight in the air with her finger.

Miss Crump scowled. "I fail to see the humor in that, Olivia."

You can always tell how annoyed Miss Crump is by how many wrinkles she gets in her forehead. I counted one, two, three wrinkles, thanks to Lovey.

"Sit down, Olivia," she said through gritted teeth.

Lovey seemed to have messed up Miss Crump's train of thought, because instead of moving on to division, she started to clean her desk. Bad news for Lovey, because that's another sure sign that Miss Crump is annoyed.

As often as Miss Crump gets annoyed, you'd think her desk would be spotless. Think again. Mostly she just shuffles her mess around. The truth is, no one has actually ever seen her desk under the mountain of papers and books and craft

supplies. Now and then Miss Crump tosses her attendance book onto the pile and accidentally starts an avalanche. She has to throw her body across the top to hold everything in place. Sometimes it works, though usually a pencil holder or coffee mug crashes to the floor.

Without even a tiny smile from Miss Crump, Lovey sighed and slumped down in her seat. She looked at me and Jeffrey and shrugged. Poor Lovey, defeated already. Pretending to rub my forehead with my finger and thumb, I was really showing Lovey an "L" for "Loser." I hope she's better on the balance beam than she is at joke telling, if she wants to win that Olympic medal.

"Complete these multiplication problems," said Miss Crump as she passed out math sheets. "Tomorrow there will be a quiz."

Everyone groaned. I passed a sheet to Alana. She took it and went straight to work. I stared at the numbers, unable to concentrate. Two things kept going through my head: the bet and Alana. This could be my chance to win both.

Chapter 6

I started to write answers to the math problems:

9	7	6	9
x 9	x 8	·x 5	x 4
elefanT	spagetti and meatballs	Thursday	dirty socks

Hey, this is funny! I thought, and could hardly keep myself from cracking up right then and there. Maybe Lovey's educational joke bombed, but mine was original. If Miss Crump really wanted to "encourage originality," she would have to prove it by laughing.

I watched her collect pens, pencils, and markers scattered around her desk, and cram them into an empty paint jar. I think she was still annoyed after Lovey's joke, because a wrinkle or two still ran across her forehead. Beads of sweat formed over my lip. My ears felt hot. I looked at my worksheet. This was a bad idea. I erased all the goofy answers, and filled in the correct ones.

9	7	6	9
x 9	x 8	x 5	x 4
81	56	30	36

Alana had already finished the problems and her nose was now planted in her comic book. She must have gotten to a funny part, because the little dimple appeared on her cheek. If only I could get her face to do that, too.

I looked over at Jeffrey. He pulled the sardine sandwich from his desk and waved it at me.

I rubbed my eraser over the answers again. By now, the smudges on the paper looked like muddy shoe prints. I knew I couldn't miss my chance, so once more, I wrote in the spaces:

9	7	6	9
x 9	x 8	x 5	x 4
elefant	spagetti and meatballs	Thursday	Dirty socks

I sat up straight and grinned. In a few minutes, Miss Crump would be collecting our papers to grade them during silent reading.

I imagined her getting to mine…She reads my first funny answer and her mouth turns up at the sides. I'm the only one who notices since everyone else is reading. A moment later, the kids hear something and look up at Miss Crump. Was that a laugh? Impossible! It must have been a hiccup, they figure, and go back to reading. They hear it again. At first it sounds like a snort but soon Miss Crump is slapping her leg and hee-hawing like a donkey. It's a miracle! After school, my classmates carry me around the

schoolyard like a champion.
Alana cheers and rewards me
with a big, dimpled smile…

"Has everyone completed the worksheet?" Miss Crump said at last, snapping me out of my daydream.

Time to pass in our papers. My heart started to race. I was going to win the dare and a dimple, all at the same time.

"Now we'll go over the answers together," said Miss Crump. "Everyone will check his or her own work."

Chapter 7

No fair! Miss Crump would never even read my answers. I groaned and went limp in my chair.

"Who would like to answer the first problem?"

I raised my hand. It wasn't over yet.

She called on Lucia. She called on Corrie. She called on Evan. Finally, only one problem remained.

"Nine times four?" Miss Crump looked straight at me as I wildly waved my arm. "Frank?"

This is it, I thought. I'll either win the bet, or get in big trouble trying.

"Dirty socks!"

"Correct, thirty six."

Huh? No—that's not what I said! Dirty socks! I said dirty socks! I wanted to yell it out, but I was too stunned to say anything. I looked around the room. No one had even flinched. Even the other kids thought I said thirty-six.

"Please put away your math books and take out your readers," said Miss Crump.

I wanted to bang my head on the desk for such a dumb mess-up. The only good thing was that Lovey and Jeffrey didn't realize what happened. If they didn't know I had used up my one and only chance, I wasn't about to tell them. At least I was still in the game.

With Lovey out of the bet, only Jeffrey and I still competed. I have to admit, I didn't think I had much of a chance against Jeffrey. After all, he's the funniest kid in the third grade. Once, when our music teacher, Mrs. Jocum, stepped out into the hall, Jeffrey actually danced the Hokey Pokey right on top of her desk!

Mrs. Jocum walked in just as he put his backside in and shook it all about. She smiled a tight smile and clapped for him. "Bravo, Jeffrey! Now take your act to Mr. Kropp's office. I'm sure he'll be amused."

Red-faced, Jeffrey dragged himself to the principal's office. Mrs. Jocum covered her mouth and tried to disguise a laugh with a fake cough. She didn't fool us. With a name that sounds like "joke-em," she had to have a sense of humor.

Miss Crump, however, wasn't like Mrs. Jocum. She had the sense of humor of a bowl of broccoli.

During silent reading Jeffrey finally decided to make his move. He crossed his arm over his mouth, with his elbow jutting out in front of his face like a pointy-nosed fox.

I gasped. Lovey saw him, too. She stared at him with big

owl eyes. Alana looked up from her book, and a faint grin appeared on her face.

Miss Crump sat at her desk grading spelling worksheets. The room was so quiet you could hear her red marker squeak across the papers.

Jeffrey's eyes darted around the room. He took a deep breath.

PFFFFT!

The whole class broke out in giggles and howls. All except Miss Crump.

One, two, three, FOUR wrinkles on her forehead. Bad news for Jeffrey.

"Go see if Mr. Kropp finds that as funny as does the rest of the class," she said, handing him

a pass to the principal's office.

Jeffrey sat there stunned. His mouth fell open, like, how could anyone not laugh at an arm fart?

Miss Crump's eyes narrowed and she pointed to the door. "Mr. Kropp's office. Now!"

I would've shown him the "L," but I didn't have the heart.

Chapter 8

By the time we lined up for gym, Lovey and I started to worry. Jeffrey still hadn't returned.

"I sure hope Mr. Kropp found the humor in Jeffrey's prank," Lovey said.

It was possible. After all, Mr. Kropp wears cartoon ties to school every day. And once a month, on Library Day, he dresses as a character in a story when he reads to the kindergarteners.

On the other hand, there was the time Blaine Davenport wrapped himself in toilet paper and walked through the hall like a mummy. Mr. Kropp didn't even chuckle. Instead, he said something about wasting school resources and made Blaine bring a new roll of toilet paper to school to replace it. He's a pretty tough guy to predict, I guess. So there's no telling what was going on right now in his office.

We were playing a game of kickball in gym class when Jeffrey ran out on the field.

"What happened?" Lovey asked, grabbing his shoulders. She's never been sent to the principal's office. She thinks there's some kind of torture chamber in there. Jeffrey lowered his voice. "It's kind of embarrassing to talk about."

"Wow, what did he do to you?" I asked.

"He didn't actually do anything to me," Jeffrey said. "It's just that…"

He stopped and looked away, gulping like he was fighting tears.

"That what?" I was sort of afraid to hear the answer.

Jeffrey took a deep breath. "…that no one ever beat me in an arm fart contest before." He laughed and punched my arm.

"A contest?" Lovey asked, "With Mr. Kropp?"

"Yeah, but it wasn't a fair one. He has five kids at home so he gets way more practice than

I do."

"True," I agreed. "That doesn't sound fair at all."

"And if that's not bad enough, he gave me a detention and said I have to apologize to Miss Crump for making rude noises in class."

"Ouch," I said sympathetically.

"When I told him I only did it because Miss Crump doesn't know how to laugh, Mr. Kropp said, 'Oh, you'd be surprised.' Then he got real weird and started reciting bad poetry."

"Poetry?" Lovey raised her eyebrows.

Jeffrey cleared his throat, and recited the poem in a pretty good imitation of Mr. Kropp's voice:

"Miss Crump is prone
to enter the zone
when you can tickle
her funny bone."

"Yep. That is bad poetry," said Lovey.

"What's a funny bone?" I asked. They both shrugged.

Then Lovey wagged a finger at me. "Hey Frankie, Jeffrey and I might have lost, but you haven't won yet either."

"Yeah, Frankie," said Jeffrey. "What's your plan?"

I already tried my one good idea, and didn't want to admit I had no more.

"Maybe I can find Miss Crump's funny bone and tickle it," I said. "I could sneak up behind her with a feather or something."

Jeffrey thought about it and nodded. "Might work. Nothing

makes me laugh harder than being tickled until I practically wet my pants."

"My sister and I play Tickle War," added Lovey. "We use a stopwatch to see how long I can take it before giving up."

"Bet you wish it was an Olympic sport so you could get a medal," said Jeffrey.

Lovey smiled. "My best time is four minutes, sixteen seconds. I'm working on a full five minutes."

"Mom doesn't let Dad tickle me anymore," I said. "Not since the time he tickled me after dinner, and I puked up my ravioli."

Lovey made a gross-out

face. Soon Mr. Sidney, the gym teacher, called her up for her turn to kick the ball.

"Do you really think Miss Crump might be ticklish?" Jeffrey asked.

For a minute I imagined Miss Crump playing Tickle War, snorting and giggling as she rolled around on the classroom floor.

"Not a chance." I sighed.

I decided it would be bad news to try to tickle Miss Crump anyway. She's real big on "keeping one's hands to oneself."

Chapter 9

After gym, we returned to class. With less than two hours until the last bell, I hadn't come up with a sure way to get a laugh out of Miss Crump. I could almost taste Jeffrey's disgusting sardine sandwich.

I smacked my head, trying to jolt my brain into coming up

with a funny idea. I thought about how comic books made Alana laugh. Right now, she had one hidden inside her open science book while she pretended to read about volcanoes.

Maybe I could draw a comic strip about our class. Not only could that make Miss Crump laugh, she might even give me credit for an "extracurricular activity." That's her way of saying "more work."

Most of my colored pencils had broken points. I grabbed a fistful of them, and headed for the sharpener.

"Where are you going, Frank?" said Miss Crump.

"To sharpen some pencils."

"We don't need pencils to discuss volcanoes. Please return to your seat."

Busted. I plopped back in my chair and began drawing my cartoon, *Miss Crump, Superhero*, in pink and green. None of the other colors had sharp enough points. I figured Miss Crump might find the cartoon funny as long as I made her the hero. Her character wore a flowing math worksheet cape while she taught multiplication in front of a class full of broccoli.

"Frank, you're not attentive today. Is there something you find more interesting than lava

flow?" She stood glaring at me with her hands on her hips, exactly like in my cartoon. Alana looked up from her comic book and over at my drawing.

"No, Ma'am."

Miss Crump kept her eyes on me until I slipped the paper inside my desk. Jeffrey and Lovey watched me, too, with little smirks on their faces. Without a chance to finish the comic strip, I'd need a new plan.

Think, think, think...What's the funniest thing I ever saw? The only thing that popped into my head was my dad in his SpongeBob boxer shorts. Even Miss Crump would have to laugh at that. Of course, since Dad wasn't likely to show up to my class in his underwear, that idea didn't help much at all. Still, I made a mental note to take a picture of him one of these days.

"Class, please take out your homework notebook," Miss Crump said.

I looked at the clock—only ten minutes left before the bell. I realized I had run out of ideas, or as Mr. Picaso would say, "my muse took a snooze."

I hated to admit that it was time to throw in the towel. With a three-way tie for last place, we'd all have to share Jeffrey's smelly sardine sandwich.

I tore a sheet of paper from my notebook and scribbled a note to Jeffrey:

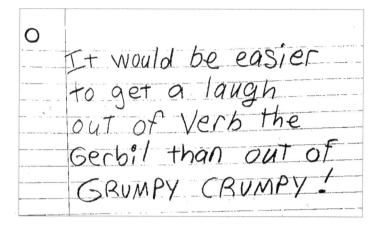

It would be easier
to get a laugh
out of Verb the
Gerbil than out of
GRUMPY CRUMPY!

At the bottom of the note, I drew a picture of Miss Crump in SpongeBob boxer shorts and crayons sticking out of her nose.

I folded the note into a paper airplane. When Miss Crump turned to the board to write our homework assignment, I flew it over to Jeffrey. As he read it, he covered his mouth to hold in a laugh, and a big old snort came out instead.

Miss Crump spun around. Jeffrey quickly folded the note and shoved it under his thigh.

Too late.

"Jeffrey, please share the joke with the class," Miss Crump said.

Jeffrey nervously held up the crinkled note.

"And from whom did you get that?" Miss Crump rolled the chalk between her fingers.

Jeffrey looked down at the floor and said nothing.

"I gave it to him," I mumbled.

Miss Crump stepped up to my desk and cupped her hand behind her ear. "What did you say?" she asked, though I'm

pretty sure she heard it the first time.

"It was me. I passed him the note," I said louder.

"Jeffrey, put that on my desk," said Miss Crump, though I didn't think there was room on the mound for one more sliver of paper. "And Franklin, you will stay in your seat after the bell rings."

Very bad news for me.

She turned back to the board too fast for me to count the wrinkles in her forehead.

Chapter 10

"Take out a sheet of paper, Franklin," Miss Crump said. We were nearly alone now, and her eyes burned into mine. "You're going to write an essay on why you won't pass notes in class."

That wasn't the worst part of the punishment. Today Alana

was staying after school to straighten the book shelf. She would see the whole embarrassing thing—and she heard Miss Crump call me 'Franklin.' I wanted to crawl under my desk.

I tried not to look over at the folded note. It lay nestled on the desk between a stack of colored construction paper and a painted wooden apple with a broken clock in its side.

Maybe she'd forget about it. Maybe she wouldn't see it drowning in the mess on her desk. Maybe I could sneak it back when she wasn't looking. For now, though, her forehead remained surprisingly wrinkle-free. I decided to play it safe, and started to write my essay while she wiped the board clean.

> *I will not pass not pass notes in class. Passing notes is rude. Passing notes is distracting to the class.*

I stopped writing when I saw Miss Crump put down her eraser. She turned away from the board and lowered herself onto her chair. My heart thumped in my chest. She seemed to move in slow motion, the way they do in scary movies when something bad is about to happen. I could even hear that creepy-movie music in my head.

And then, as if she had some kind of radar, she reached straight for the note.

Alana saw it, too. She watched with a look of pity on her face. Instead of getting a dimple from her, I got pity. How much worse could this day get?

"I'm done, Miss Crump," she blurted.

FACTS ARE FUN
CHECK THEM REGULARLY

NEATNESS COUNTS

Miss Crump looked up from her desk. "Thank you, Alana. You may leave now."

For a minute Alana didn't move. She glanced at the note in Miss Crump's hand, and then at me. "Okay, bye!" She grabbed her backpack and darted from the room. I felt relieved that she wouldn't see Miss Crump call the principal and my parents and the entire PTA, once she read my note.

I gulped as Miss Crump slowly unfolded the paper. My palms started to sweat. I stared at her forehead, betting on at least five wrinkles. That would be a new record.

But, rather than lines
appearing on her forehead, I saw
little creases form on the sides of
her eyes. At the same time, her
lips curled up at the corners. I
thought maybe she was going to
be sick again.

Instead, a weird thing happened. She tilted back her head, and let out a real, loud, genuine LAUGH!

It sounded like music.

Miss Crump looked straight at me. "Grumpy Crumpy? That's a good one!" She laughed again. "You know, when I was your age, my big brother called me 'Plumpy Crumpy.' I tell you—I didn't like that one at all."

Not knowing what to say, I mumbled, "Yeah, that's mean." Though I wasn't sure how "Grumpy Crumpy" sounded any better.

"Oh, he paid for it alright," she snickered. "Whenever our father heard him tease me, he got spanked on his bottom." She paused for effect, holding back another laugh before adding, "Yes, brother *Crump* got a *thump* on his *rump!*"

She howled again, and for a moment seemed to forget I was even there.

A second later she leaned closer to me and kind of whispered, "Bet you can't guess what Principal Kropp calls my desk."

Her eyes twinkled. Mine got wide. This I had to hear.

"What?"

"The Crump Dump!"

We both laughed till our sides hurt. Miss Crump howled so hard that tears rolled out of her eyes. *Oh man!* I thought. *If only she'd been drinking milk!*

She finally caught her breath and smiled at me. "Wow," she said.

That's all…"wow." That one word said a lot.

Maybe Miss Crump's not so bad, I decided. Who would have guessed her to be a sucker for goofy rhymes?

Then as quickly as it came, her smile disappeared. She cleared her throat and motioned to the essay on my desk. "Now finish up," she said.

Miss Crump turned away and gathered up class work to grade at home. She slipped the papers into her briefcase right on top of a fat book called "Zany Limericks from Around the World."

Chapter 11

Did it really happen? If her cheeks weren't still wet from tears, I might have wondered if I imagined the whole thing.

When I gave her my essay, she looked it over and nodded. She shook the paper in front of my face, eyed me sternly, and said, "I hope you've learned something from this."

I sure did. Even Grumpy Crumpy has a laugh inside her waiting to come out.

As for winning the bet, how would I explain this to Jeffrey and Lovey? There's no way they would ever believe me. I could hardly believe it myself, and I was there! I figured I'd better get ready to face that sardine sandwich—and that would be nothing to laugh about.

I picked up my books and moved toward the classroom door. Looking back at Miss Crump, I knew things were going to be different. I was sure that good laugh had changed her forever, and she would have a sense of humor from now on.

I smiled and waved. "Bye, Grumpy Crumpy!"

Her eyes narrowed. Her lips tightened. "Excuse me?"

Oops. I guess I was wrong. "Nothing. See you tomorrow."

I ran from the room—smack into Alana, who had been standing outside the door.

"Were you here the whole time?" I asked.

She nodded. "I saw her go for the note. I had to know what she was going to do to you."

"So you heard it? You heard her laugh?" I studied Alana's face. Her eyes met mine, and it seemed as if she were seeing me for the first time.

"Oh, I heard it alright!" And next thing I knew, that little dimple popped right into her cheek. Her grin spread wider until a second dimple appeared on the other cheek. I felt like I won the lottery. Even if no one else ever believed what happened today, I still won a double-dimple smile from Alana Song!

Together we made our way down the hall. "Hey, will you tell Jeffrey and Lovey what happened in there?" I asked. "They'll never believe me."

"Only if you do something for me," she said.

I stopped in my tracks and frowned. She wore that same look Jeffrey gets when he makes a wild dare. "Will it land me in Mr. Kropp's office?" I asked.

"Of course not," said Alana. She looped her arm through mine and we stepped out into the school yard. "I just want you to promise to finish your *Miss Crump, Superhero* comic

strip. I saw it from my desk. It looks pretty funny."

For Alana, I'd draw an entire comic book. "Sure! I'll get right on it."

Anything to tickle her funny bone.

ABOUT THE AUTHOR

Rachelle Burk is a writer of fiction, nonfiction, and poetry for children. Her work has appeared in national publications such as *Highlights for Children* and *Scholastic Science World* classroom magazines.

Rachelle is a popular children's entertainer, performing as "Mother Goof Storyteller" and "Tickles the Clown." In a parallel life, she works as a social worker and rescue squad volunteer.

The New Jersey author loves to share the joy of reading and writing through dynamic **School Author Visit** programs. For more information, visit her website:

www.rachelleburk.com

Other Books by
Rachelle Burk

Tree House in a Storm (picture book)

Don't Turn the Page! (picture book)

Sleep Soundly at Beaver's Inn (picture book)

The Tooth Fairy Trap (chapter book)

The Walking Fish (middle grade novel)

Painting in the Dark: Esref Armagan,
Blind Artist (picture book biography)